W9-API-444

HILLTOP ELEMENTARY SCHOOL

AUDREY WOOD · MARK TEAGUE
THE
FLYING DRAGON ROOM

1861418

The Blue Sky Press / An Imprint of Scholastic Inc. / New York

HILLTOP ELEMENTARY SCHOOL

For Bruce Robert Wood — A.W.

For Lily — M.T.

Text copyright © 1996 by Audrey Wood   Illustrations copyright © 1996 by Mark Teague

All rights reserved.
No part of this publication may be reproduced or stored in a retrieval system or transmitted in
any form or by any means, electronic, mechanical, photocopying, recording, or otherwise,
without written permission of the publisher.

For information regarding permission, please write to: Permissions Department,
The Blue Sky Press, an imprint of Scholastic Inc., 555 Broadway, New York, New York 10012.

The Blue Sky Press is a trademark of Scholastic Inc.

Cataloging-in-Publication Data available   Library of Congress number: 95-15301

ISBN 0-590-48193-2 (h.c.)   CIP   AC

12 11 10 9 8 7 6 5 4 3 2 1   6 7 8 9/9 0 1/0

Printed in Singapore   First printing, March 1996
The illustrations in this book were done with acrylics.
Production supervision by Angela Biola   Designed by Claire Counihan

THE BLUE SKY PRESS

HILLTOP ELEMENTARY SCHOOL

It all happened because of

the Flying Dragon Room, or so they say, though Patrick didn't know that at first.

It was summer, and Patrick's mother and father had hired Mrs. Jenkins to help them paint the house. Patrick wanted to help paint, too, but his parents just thought he would get in the way.

That's when Mrs. Jenkins brought out her special tools. "I just built something fun with these," she said. "Why don't you borrow them and see what you can make?"

All that week, while the house was being painted, Patrick worked in the backyard with Mrs. Jenkins' special tools. On Saturday, he invited everyone, including Baby Sarah, over to see his new place.

"Get ready for the backyard surprise of your life," he said. "Mrs. Jenkins gets to push the invisible button."

Mrs. Jenkins did. A door in the ground opened slowly.

Everyone followed Patrick down the steps, through a dark tunnel, and into a large cavern.

"Welcome to the Subterranean Room," Patrick said.

"Step right this way for a tour of the Small Creature Garden!"

"Eee gads!" Mother exclaimed. "What are those creepy-crawly things?"

"Don't worry, Mom," Patrick said as he handed her one. "They wouldn't hurt a flea."

"Where does that go?" Father asked, pointing to a strange ladder.

"To get to the next room," Patrick explained, "we must climb the Zig-Zaggity-Ladder."

"Welcome to the Bubble Room," Patrick said.

Mrs. Jenkins peeked through an enormous bubble. "What's that gizmo over there?" she asked.

"That," Patrick explained, "is my Bigger-Better-Bubble-Blower. It never quits unless I say" (then he whispered), "ubble, ubble, no ubbly bubs!"

"Oh, no!" Mother cried. "Where is Baby Sarah?"

"Follow me," Patrick said. "I know where she went."

"Welcome to the Food Room," he said. "There's plenty for all, help yourself."

The hungry travelers gathered treats of every kind, then sat down to eat.

When they finished, Patrick pulled on a monkey chain.
"Presto!" he shouted. "It's the Snake Slide!"

"Welcome to the Jumping Room!" Patrick cried. "Jump up and down, scream all you want. That's what you do in the Jumping Room!"

"Whoopee!" Mrs. Jenkins shouted as she did a back flip with a twist. Father tried belly scoops, Mom pretended she could fly, and Baby Sarah jumped clear out of sight!

"Now hear this!" Patrick announced on his Mega-Mega-Phone. "Jump aboard the *Jolly Mermaid*. It's time to sail!"

Grasping the wheel, Patrick steered the *Jolly Mermaid* through the dark waters.

"Oh, no!" Mother cried. "What's that?"

Frothing water began to swirl around the boat. Fire and vapors shot up from the salty depths.

"It looks like we're in for a rough crossing," Mrs. Jenkins said.

"Emergency!" Patrick shouted. "Hang on for dear life! The Underwater Fire Lizard is surfacing!"

The clawed hand of a giant sea monster reached for the
Jolly Mermaid. Patrick threw open Mrs. Jenkins' toolbox
and took out a measuring stick.
   Pointing it at the creature, he shouted, "Water Lizard!
Fire Worm! X, Apostrophe, S! Shrink! Shrink! Shrink!"

As the shrinking sea monster tumbled through the air, Patrick reached out and caught it. "Another fine specimen for my Small Creature Garden," he said.

"Hurray!" Father cheered, giving his son a hug.

"Patrick is our hero!" Mother agreed, kissing him on the cheek.

"This is the best adventure I've had in years!" Mrs. Jenkins said.

The *Jolly Mermaid* sailed peacefully up a river and into a lush lagoon.

"Emergency!" Father cried. "We're surrounded by giant, people-eating alligators!"

"Don't worry, Dad," Patrick said. "They're friends of mine. Welcome to the Friendly Wild Animal Room!" he shouted.

All the friendly wild animals gathered around. Mother braided a buffalo's curly locks, Father tickled a giraffe's chin, and Baby Sarah snuggled up with a napping lion.

"Is that a Tyrannosaurus rex over there?" Mrs. Jenkins wanted to know.

"Yep!" Patrick said. "Give her some carrots, Mrs. Jenkins. She likes them!"

"Why, she's just tame as a kitten," Mrs. Jenkins said. "I like your place, Patrick."

"There's no place like my place," he agreed.

"Perhaps," Mrs. Jenkins said with a wink, "but you haven't seen my place yet."

"Your place?!" Patrick exclaimed.

"Yep," she said. "Everyone's invited to my place
tomorrow morning." Mrs. Jenkins blew on her whistle,
then picked up her special toolbox.

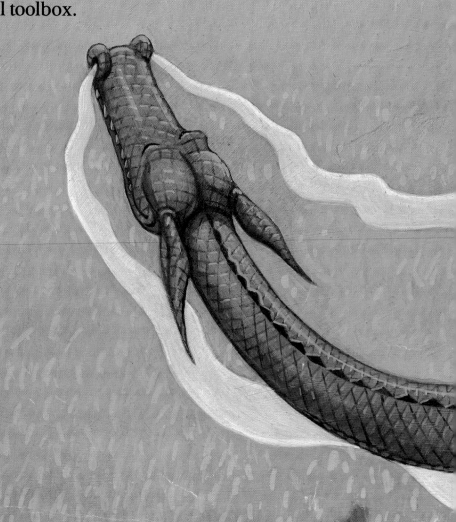

"Don't be late," she called. "The tour begins at ten
o'clock in my Flying Dragon Room."
And it did, or so they say.